EYEWITNESS

GRUESOME HISTORIES

Written by Susan Mayes

Illustrated by Celia Witchard

HENDERSON

An imprint of DK Publishing, Inc.
Copyright © 1997 Dorling Kindersley Ltd.

A WORD OF WARNING

Is your knowledge of the past everything it could be? Do you hunger for the details behind all those dull dates and events?

This book contains a grim feast of delightfully unpleasant facts that didn't quite make it into your school textbooks, but maybe should have!

A word of warning...avoid eating and drinking while devouring gruesome historical information; it could damage your health, not to mention the new carpet!

Just to give you an idea of what to expect, here's a little taste of things to come...

The Romans may have been pioneering and powerful people, but some of their habits seem a bit nasty by today's standards. Find out about life in the public bathroom and after-dinner puking!

Discover the delights that awaited girls in ancient Greece – providing they were not abandoned at birth, that is!

Preserved bodies, otherwise known as mummies, will keep you riveted to the spot. Read about *natural* mummies and about the not-so-natural. Ooh-er!

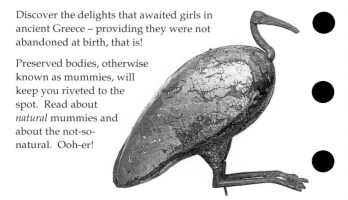

Enter the grisly world of old-fashioned medicine, but only if you are feeling strong and reckless. Definitely not one for the squeamish!

What was life like at sea? Is there any truth behind the tales of pillaging pirates, maggot-infested food, and rat-ridden ships? (Ahoy, lad!)

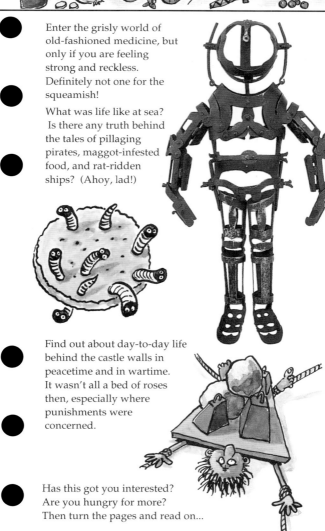

Find out about day-to-day life behind the castle walls in peacetime and in wartime. It wasn't all a bed of roses then, especially where punishments were concerned.

Has this got you interested? Are you hungry for more? Then turn the pages and read on...

Early Nasties

An archaeologist is someone who studies ancient things...and we're talking a teeny bit more ancient than your grandma! Well, quite a lot more ancient actually.

Here are a few of the not-so-nice things that archaeologists have found out about people who lived long before us.

What a Way to Go!

Many thousands of years ago, in ancient societies, dying was an important business. Some civilizations built a funeral pyre – that's a big bonfire – and put the dead body on top. Then the whole thing was burned, accompanied by the odd sacrificial victim or two. Nice, huh? Afterward, the bones might have been laid to rest in a burial chamber, along with a few essentials for the dead person to use in the afterlife. (Well, you never know what you might need!)

Funeral pyre

A TIGHT SQUEEZE

Human remains have been found buried inside huge clay jars, of all things. Not the most comfortable resting place you could imagine!

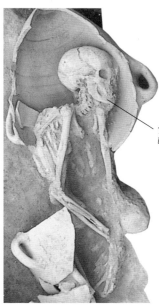

This skeleton was found buried in a jar in Jordan.

WHAT A SMELL!

In the past, on the islands of the South Pacific, a substance called *ambergris* was used as a basis for perfumes. It was made from the intestines of the sperm whale and had a strong scent!

SWEET BREATH

If you had bad breath, frankincense (the resin from a type of spruce tree) was the thing to take. Who needs a refreshing packet of strong mints?

Frankincense

HORRID ROMAN HABITS

The ancient Romans were around from 753 BC, for about 1,163 years. They were powerful, intelligent people who did lots of good things, but they had a few horrid habits that you really MUST know about.

At Your Convenience

Plumbing was one of the Romans' strong points. They built public restrooms where multiseat toilets were placed over a water channel, with running water to wash the waste to the public sewer.

In those days, they didn't have toilet paper. They used a stick with a piece of sponge on the end!

A Day Out

For a fun day in Roman times you could take a trip to Rome and go to the Colosseum – a big building used for entertainment and sports. One of the highlights in this 50,000-seat stadium was when trained fighters called gladiators fought each other to the death, for public amusement.

Gladiator's helmet

MEALTIME

The Romans loved their meals. The rich ones in particular spent hours over their main meal. It was polite to belch during a good feed, and they HAD to eat with their hands, because they didn't have forks. Sounds ideal!

SICKY-ICKY

There was often so much food around at Roman meals, that the only way to get through it all was to make yourself sick to make space for another helping. Some houses had a special room called a *vomitorium*, where you could go to puke in peace. The other option was to vomit on the floor. Uuuugh!

ROMAN REVENGE

If you had an enemy in Roman times, you could seek revenge by visiting your nearest temple and placing a curse on them.

This curse is written on a lead plaque.

ERUPTION AND DESTRUCTION

One of the most famous gruesome tales is about the destruction of the Italian cities of Pompeii and Herculaneum. They were buried when the nearby volcano Mount Vesuvius erupted in AD 79.

On August 24, AD 79, people in Pompeii and the nearby city of Herculaneum were going about their daily business...eating, shopping, taking a nap.

Without warning, Vesuvius erupted and buried Pompeii under several feet of volcanic ash. Herculaneum was swamped by volcanic mud that was 65 ft (20 m) deep in places. That's five times more than covered Pompeii.

Volcanic ash rained down on Pompeii for several hours.

GRUESOME FINDS

The buried cities of Pompeii and Herculaneum were more or less forgotten until excavations started in the 18th century. Little by little, the remains were revealed. Many gruesome finds tell the tale of what happened during those terrifying hours all those years ago.

One poor guard dog was chained to his post when disaster struck.

One person was found sitting huddled, covering his face in his last moments of life.

This mother was trying to shield her child when they died.

Body cavity is discovered.

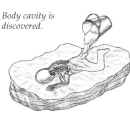

Cavity is filled with wet plaster of Paris.

PLASTER CASTS

Human and animal remains were not found complete. Over the years, the bodies decayed, leaving shapes where they used to be inside the hardened volcanic rock.

When archaeologists discovered the cavities, they filled them with plaster to make solid shapes of what used to be inside.

A GRISLY GREEK BEGINNING

Growing up in ancient Greece wasn't a bundle of laughs. The life of a child was a bit of an ordeal, especially when there was a good chance that you wouldn't be allowed to live. Yikes!

NEW BABIES

A baby's future rested in the hands of its father. If it was a girl or if it was puny, or if the family was poor, it might be abandoned and left in the open air to die!

A few abandoned babies were lucky and were saved by other families and brought up as slaves. If a baby was accepted by its own family and named on the tenth day of its life, it was treated kindly. Phew!

BELIEVE IT OR NOT...

Children were considered to be young adults at about the age of 12 or 13. They had to dedicate their toys to the god Apollo or the goddess Artemis. This was the sign that they had reached the end of childhood.

Clay toys

A Boy's Life

Boys went to school at about 7 years of age. Each had a personal slave called a pedagogue to carry their books!

At school they learned reading, writing, and arithmetic, plus music. So far, so good, but... they had to learn lots of poetry by heart and learn to discuss subjects in an interesting and intelligent way. This was called debating. Uh-oh!

A Girl's Life

Greek girls were not as important as the boys. They didn't go to school; they stayed at home where mom taught them to spin, weave, and take care of the house. (Big deal!)

A few richer girls might have been taught to read and write by a personal tutor.

Girls married at 13 or 14. A girl's father chose her husband and the only way she could gain even a little importance would be to have a baby boy. Huh!

BEASTLY BODIES

The preserved bodies of people or animals are called *mummies*. If people die or are buried in the right conditions, they may be mummified by accident. Mummies still have skin on them, so skeletons don't count.

For the brave and strong-stomached only! Do NOT read this while eating your lunch!

Mummy of Eskimo baby

DEEP FREEZE

When someone dies, invisible little nasties called bacteria make the body decay or, to put it another way, rot. But if bodies are buried in very cold, icy places, they become frozen, so decay never starts.

The six-month-old Eskimo baby on the left died around 1475. His body lay protected from the sun and snow and was freeze-dried by the Arctic air.

One frozen mummy, found in its icy coffin in 1984, probably died about 140 years earlier, in the freezing Canadian Arctic. Gruesome, eh?

BOG PEOPLE

Peatbogs are wet, earthy places that are perfect for preserving bodies. This is because there isn't any of the oxygen that bacteria need to make things decay.

Tollund Man was the name given to a natural mummy found in a Danish peatbog. The body is more than 2,200 years old, but it is perfectly preserved.

SAND MUMMY

The earliest known Egyptian mummies are around 5,000 years old. Wow...that's some old person!

The dead body was buried in a shallow hole in the desert and covered with sand. This mummified the body really well. The sand mummy in this picture still has her hair. She is known as Gingerella!

GOOD LUCK MUMMIES

In 16th- and 17th-century England, builders used to board up a dead animal in the house they were finishing, along with a few lucky bits and pieces. The cold drafts often freeze-dried the dead offering and mummified it.

MAKING A MUMMY

The Egyptians believed in life after death, or the *afterlife*. They wanted to preserve a dead person's body in a lifelike way to prepare him or her for a better future life. Here's how they did it.

EMBALMING

First, remove all the vital organs, except the heart, which may be needed in the next world. Wash the body in wine and spices, then cover with a special salt. Leave for seventy days. Then pour over liquid resin and rub in oil, wax, and other stuff to prevent cracking. Lastly, pack with linen, sand, or sawdust to achieve a good body shape.

WRAPPING UP

Next, wrap the mummy in hundreds of feet of linen cloth. Do layers of bandage alternated with large sheets of material, called shrouds. Do up to 20 layers in this way. But DON'T forget to wrap the fingers and toes individually!

THE MUMMY'S MASK

Make a decorative mask to protect the mummy's head, or to replace it if you have accidentally lost or damaged the real thing! Painted papier-mâché will do for poorer mummies, but go for gold if they are rich ones! Also add charms, called *amulets*, to protect the body from evil and to bring good luck.

MUMMY CASES

Place your completed work of art in a decorated coffin, called a mummy case, to protect it from wild animals and tomb thieves. Place in a second case, just to be on the safe side.

STONE COFFIN

Lastly, if your mummy is a VIP, place in a stone coffin, called a *sarcophagus*. There...that didn't take long, did it?

DEADLY IMPORTANCE

A *pharaoh* was an Egyptian king. The Egyptians believed that their pharaoh was a living god, so when he died they took the best possible care of him. In addition to receiving all the routine after-death perks described on pages 14 and 15, there were other delights in store.

PYRAMIDS

During a pharaoh's lifetime, he had an enormous pyramid built as a tomb and final resting place for his body. It was meant to help him achieve eternal life.

THE FUNERAL

A pharaoh's funeral was a grand affair. His mummified body was taken to the pyramid in a procession led by priests. He was accompanied by professional mourners who did loads of wailing and throwing around of sand... a bit of a show!

TAKING IT WITH YOU

Mummies were buried with their own set of useful things for the afterlife. If you were a VIP, these things might include statues, furniture, jewelry, and model workers, called *shabtis* to do all the hard work.

This pendant was buried with the famous King Tutankhamun.

THE "OPENING OF THE MOUTH" CEREMONY

This ceremony was performed to restore the mummy's senses so it could eat, drink, and generally live it up in the afterlife. The ceremony was performed by priests who touched the mummy's mouth with ritual instruments.

SPOOKY SPELLS

The ultimate Egyptian handbook was called *The Book of the Dead*. This handy little volume contained a collection of spells. Each one was a prayer or a plea from the dead person and was meant to help them on the tricky trip to the next world.

MUMMY MANIA

The Egyptians set a bit of a trend in mummification. Not only did they preserve their human loved ones, but they preserved other things besides. The fashion has been continued over the centuries, with some pretty weird results.

MUMMIFIED CATS & DOGS

The Egyptians kept cats as pets. They were sacred animals and anyone who killed a cat could be punished with death. (Yikes!) Some families took their cats to be embalmed when they passed on. Even dead wild dogs got special treatment.

Mummy of a wild dog

BELIEVE IT OR NOT...

When a cat died, the owners may have shaved their eyebrows. Why?

As a mark of respect, of course!

ANIMALS OF IMPORTANCE

The Egyptians believed that different animals were the representatives of different gods. If you thought that mummified cats and dogs were weird, take a look at this collection.

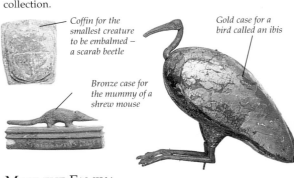

Coffin for the smallest creature to be embalmed – a scarab beetle

Gold case for a bird called an ibis

Bronze case for the mummy of a shrew mouse

MEET THE FAMILY

In Sicily, there are about 6,000 mummies in an underground cemetery, called a *catacomb*. The oldest ones are nearly 400 years old.

In the past, families took their children to visit their long-dead great-grandparents. They had a comfortable chat with the dead and even took a picnic to eat outside. You can still visit the mummies today.

FISHY FRAUD

Imaginary creatures called *mermaids* and *mermen* were popular in 17th-century Europe. The mummified merman in this picture was given to an English prince by someone who claimed that it had been caught by a Japanese fisherman. Hmmm! It was REALLY made from a monkey's head and a fish's tail.

CREEPY CURES

Back in ancient times, when people didn't know a lot about the causes of illness, there were some pretty odd cures around. It's a wonder people survived at all when you look at some of the remedies they came up with.

HEAD HOLES

In Stone Age times, they developed a nifty little medical routine for releasing the evil spirits and demons that caused mental problems and other illnesses. It was called *trepanning* and involved drilling a hole in the head to let the demons out. Ouch! An aspirin gets my vote every time!

Trepanned skull with three holes

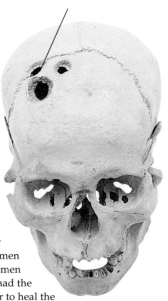

MEDICINE MEN

North American Indians had doctors called *shamans*. They

were men or women who had the power to heal the sick. If you were feeling a bit sick, the shaman would prepare herbal remedies and conduct a dramatic ceremony to promote healing. Just what the doctor ordered!

MAGIC AND MEDICINE

In Egyptian times, doctors and magicians worked together to cure some problems. A mixture of medicines and spells were used if the patient had a snake or scorpion bite. Magic alone could be used to help prevent possible injury from a hungry crocodile.

LITTLE REMINDERS

The Romans used to ask the gods to cure their illnesses. They left models of the body part they were having problems with to remind the gods of the cure they had asked for. The mind boggles!

PREVENTIVE MEDICINE

Roman soldiers were fed a daily ration of garlic to keep them healthy. Imagine the smell as the army approached. It's no wonder that the Romans conquered so many countries!

Garlic

Fenugreek
(used for
treating
pneumonia)

Mustard was
thought to have
healing properties.

"Now This Won't Hurt..."

Does the sight of a needle make your tummy turn over? Well, this little assortment of historical medical procedures will have it heaving in no time! Rest assured – they were the "in thing" at the time they were practiced.

Bronze cupping vessel

CUPPING

In Roman times, they did a thing called *cupping* to draw poison from the body. Like squeezing a pimple? No...nothing as comfortable as that!

A cup with a piece of burning cloth was pressed on the skin. The burning used up all the oxygen in the cup and sucked it onto the body, drawing out all the poison.

URINE TESTING

The life of medieval doctors was not all a bundle of laughs. An important way of finding out what was wrong with a patient was to test their urine. There were up to 30 things to note, including the color, the smell, and, wait for it...the taste! Uuugh!

Blood-letting

The ancient practice of blood-letting was very popular in the Middle Ages. If you were feeling sick in any way, draining a bit of blood from the body was supposed to make you feel a whole lot better. Not so sure myself! Blood-sucking relatives of earthworms called *leeches* were used as a slow way of blood-letting. Just pop one on the skin, let it drink five times its own weight in blood (no problem for a leech), then peel it off.

Leeches

Blood Transfusions

Once it had been discovered that blood flowed around the body in a particular way, more experiments began. (Uh-oh!) They tried replacing the blood of sick people with the blood of animals. Needless to say, it didn't work.

TOOLS OF THE TRADE

Here's a gruesome little history quiz to entertain you and your friends on rainy afternoons. Look at this awesome collection of historical medical tools and decide what each one was used for.

1 (a) Early African probes for digging decayed bits from teeth
    (b) Early Chinese acupuncture needles, used to relieve health problems
    (c) Sharp thorns used by Australian Aboriginals to sew up wounds

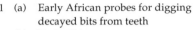

2 (a) Machine used in the 1800s for making tablets
    (b) Late 19th-century antiseptic machine
    (c) A 19th-century machine used to test urine samples

3 (a) A late Roman device for holding a wound open during surgery
    (b) An Egyptian charm pinned to clothing to ward off illness
    (c) A Roman holder for false teeth

4 (a) A 19th-century oxygen mask
    (b) A false nose
    (c) A Roman heel support

5 (a) Tool for removing tonsils
    (b) Tool for holding operating instruments in antiseptic
    (c) Tool for removing appendix

6 (a) A mechanical massager
   (b) Part of a 19th-century dental drill
   (c) Tool used to apply pressure
       to a wound to stop
       blood flow

7 (a) Tool used for ear examinations
   (b) A 19th-century
       ear syringe
   (c) Microscope for
       examining
       blood samples

8 (a) Prototype
       syringe for
       taking blood samples

   (b) Late 18th-century syringe for
       injecting cordials into the stomach
   (c) Early 19th-century stethoscope

9 (a) A 17th-century model for teaching
       bone-setting
   (b) A 17th-century frame to
       hold patients still during
       an operation
   (c) Early Chinese support to teach
       children good body posture

10 (a) A 17th-century scalpel
   (b) A 17th-century tongue depressor
       for inspecting the back of the throat
   (c) A 16th-century spatula for mixing
       and applying ointments

1 (c) 2 (b) 3 (c) 4 (b) 5 (a) 6 (c) 7 (a) 8 (c) 9 (a) 10 (b)

Answers

ODIOUS OPERATIONS

Before the mid-19th century, having an
operation was a hideous and agonizing
event – one to miss if humanly possible.
But things DID get better, thank goodness!
Here's a quick rundown on a few
operation procedures.

OPERATING WITH ANTS
In the ancient world, surgery in
India was quite a sophisticated
affair. They had some unlikely little
helpers in the form of black ants.
These made a strong antiseptic acid
and were used as clips instead
of stitches.

HAIRCUT OR OPERATION?
Until the 16th century, doctors were not well thought of.
Many surgeons combined surgery with being a barber and
had an even worse reputation. (Surprise, surprise!)
However, once they set up special training colleges, things
began to look up.

LET'S HEAR IT FOR JOSEPH LISTER
Joseph Lister (1827-1912) introduced
the use of antiseptics. This helped
prevent people from dying from
infection after operations.
Hooray!

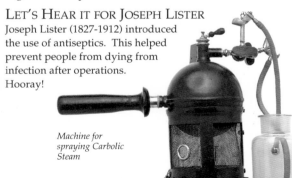

*Machine for
spraying Carbolic
Steam*

FREE FROM PAIN

There were no anesthetics before the 19th century, so people having operations had to either drink loads of alcohol, be knocked out, or faint in agony. NOT nice!

In the mid-19th century, anesthesia was developed, so patients slept during operations. Hooray, HOORAY!

Believe It or Not...

Today, a surgeon's basic tools would still be recognized by a surgeon from ancient Greece or Rome.

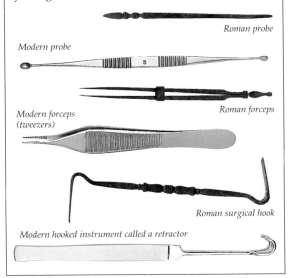

Roman probe

Modern probe

Modern forceps (tweezers)

Roman forceps

Roman surgical hook

Modern hooked instrument called a retractor

Setting Sail

About the 15th century, sailing became a popular way to explore. Later, trading ships carried cargo to different countries around the world. Life at sea wasn't all smooth sailing though. Conditions were cramped and filthy, and the sailors had to be tough.

Merchant ship

Ships' Bathrooms

A ship's bathrooms were called the *heads*, or seats of ease. They were very basic – a hole cut in the deck with a seat on top. If a sailor couldn't get to the official bathroom, he used a bucket instead. Care had to be taken when emptying it overboard!

Maggoty Cookies

Cookies featured heavily in a sailor's diet, and we're not talking nice chocolate ones either. They were rock-hard and infested with maggots and weevils, which the sailors usually ended up eating. Yuck!

Sick Sailors

Being sick on a ship was to be avoided at all costs. Medical treatment was horribly primitive and if you got injured in battle, you stood a good chance of dying from the treatment intended to save you.

Scurvy

Scurvy was a disease that caused problems including weakness, tender gums, loss of teeth, and bleeding under the skin. Mmm... nice! In 1747, it was discovered that feeding the crew with fresh fruit and vegetables packed with vitamin C helped prevent this nasty illness.

Fresh Meat

Live animals were kept on ships to provide sailors with fresh meat. Good idea...but imagine the stink!

Slave Ships

In the 17th century, seven million people were taken from Africa to work as slaves in the West Indies and America. The conditions on the slave ships that transported them were horrific, and many of the slaves died on the journey.

Getting Ratty

A ship's *hold*, where the cargo was stored, was usually crawling with rats infested with germ-carrying fleas. The rats ate the sailors' food and even gnawed through the wood of the boat!

Most ships had a population of rats.

PILLAGING PIRATES

Fierce-looking carved Viking head

Pirates lived at sea and robbed other ships. There have been pirates around ever since there were ships for them to plunder. Here are some of the things that those daring rogues got up to.

VIKING PIRATES

From the 8th to the 11th centuries, Viking ships struck terror into the hearts of northern Europeans. Viking pirates were legendary for their attacks on ships and raids on villages.

FEARSOME FIENDS

Pirates encouraged the reputation they had of being fierce and cruel. They knew that their victims would give in more easily if they were threatened with torture and death. Well, who wouldn't?

Every pirate had his own Jolly Roger design.

JOLLY ROGER

This is the famous name of the pirate flag. The skull and crossbones on a black background was a warning to the victims to surrender without a fight. A plain red flag was feared most of all – it meant that the pirates would show no mercy.

A CAREER MOVE

Many ordinary sailors became pirates. They saw piracy as a life of freedom with a chance of becoming wealthy. Hah, hah, haaaah!

WOMEN PIRATES

Piracy was for men, so if a woman wanted a stab at it, she had to disguise herself. She had to dress in men's clothes, and take up drinking and swearing.

Gold doubloon

Silver coins called pieces of eight

RULES AND REGULATIONS

Here are a few typical rules that some pirates agreed to obey:

☠ Everyone is entitled to vote and to a share of the booze.

☠ Don't play cards or games for money.

☠ Candles out by eight o'clock.

☠ No boys or women on board.

☠ Keep weapons clean.

☠ Desertion in a battle is punished with death or marooning.

KNIGHT LIFE

The life of a knight involved lots of riding around on horseback in heavy armor and being generally bold and loyal.

EARLY KNIGHTS

In the 11th century, a group of brave men became socially recognized and very important. They were called knights. These champion fellows were warriors who fought on horseback, serving the local lord, count, or duke.

STARTING YOUNG

A boy of noble birth, destined to become a knight, was sent to a nobleman's house at the age of seven to become his page.

At about 14, he became a knight's squire. Basically, this meant that he took care of the armor and horses and learned to shoot with a bow.

A good squire became a knight at the age of 21, after only 14 years of training!

KNIGHT ATTIRE

Knights wore heavy armor to protect them when fighting. Their gear changed over the centuries, but it still looks pretty uncomfortable to the modern eye.

BELIEVE IT OR NOT...

A suit of armor weighed about 44-55 lb (20-25 kg), but the knight was still able to run, lie down, and mount his horse. There was one drawback though; armor was hot...VERY hot! Phewee!

HORSE ARMOR

A knight's horse got to wear armor, too. After all, the horse was a vital and expensive piece of the knight's equipment.

TOURNAMENTS

In a tournament, two teams of knights fought a mock battle. At first, proper battle armor and weapons were used, but by the 13th century, blunted weapons were introduced. What a relief!

JOUSTING

This was a popular pursuit with knights. In a joust, two knights on horseback fought one-on-one. They used long weapons called *lances* to push each other off their horses. Ouch!

Horse's headgear

BATTLE STATIONS

There have been battles all over the world throughout time. To save you from the horror of lots of boring dates, here are some entertaining anecdotes about life in battle.

GREAT BATTLES

The great battles of history were often short. This was because it took so much effort and strength to swing the heavy swords and wield the spears that were used at the time that the fighters soon became exhausted.

BELIEVE IT OR NOT...

The longest continuous war was between a number of European countries and it lasted from 1618 to 1648. It became known as the Thirty Years' War. Imaginative, huh?

A SCARY SIGHT

The part of an army on horseback is called the cavalry. In the past, this was split into light cavalry and heavy cavalry. The light cavalry found out what the enemy was up to and chased after beaten soldiers. The heavy cavalry charged the enemy in solid lines on the battlefield. This scary sight sent many enemies running in the opposite direction.

WHOOPS!

Doing drill is when soldiers train to use weapons efficiently. Unfortunately, French soldiers in the Napoleonic era (the late 1700s) were not too good at drill. Many of them were shot by men behind them. Careless!

Rifle drill

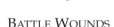

BATTLE WOUNDS

In the past, disease was a big wartime killer. Thousands of men died in battle, but thousands more died because their wounds were not properly cleaned and the operating instruments were dirty. Yuck!

IMPORTANT COLORS

A regiment's colors is the name given to its flag, with its own special design. In battle, soldiers risked their lives to protect their colors and stop the enemy from seizing them. The colors would often be passed from person to person as each bearer was shot down. Steer clear of the flag, I say!

Castle Capers

Castle-building started in the 9th and 10th centuries. Early ones were made of earth and timber; later ones were made of stone. The people who lived in a castle included the nobleman and his family, a page, a knight, a priest, and a fool (for entertainment).

Smelly Walls

When a castle was built, its walls were waterproofed with a smelly mixture of clay, animal dung, and horsehair. Perfect all-weather protection!

Castle Cuisine

Food served in a castle included meat, fish, poultry, game, eggs, vegetables, and fruit. Since they didn't have refrigerators then, some meat was salted to preserve it. Rich sauces came in handy for disguising the taste of over-ripe meat. Delicious!

Food Tasters

Before royalty or a noble family ate, a food taster had to sample each dish to check for poison. On the whole this was probably a pleasant occupation, unless you worked for an unpopular boss and wound up dead!

TOILET TROUBLES

Castle bathrooms were called *garderobes*. They either stuck out from castle walls, emptying into the moat (the watery area around the castle), or drained into a cesspool (place for collecting sewage).

HEADS OVERHEAD!

In wartime, castles were attacked by hostile armies. One of the grisly things attackers did was catapult severed heads over the castle walls. Dead animals were popular ammunition, too, since the attackers hoped to spread disease inside the castle.

The people in the castle often had their own smelly form of ammunition – human excrement!

MURDER HOLES

Holes in the roof near the main entrance of Bodiam Castle were called *murder holes*. They were used for dumping scalding water, hot sand, stones, or boiling oil on the attackers. Nice!

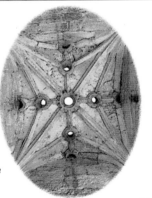

Murder holes in Bodiam Castle

GHASTLY PUNISHMENTS

Prisoners were often kept in castles. Important prisoners were treated quite well, but others were not so lucky. Here are some of the punishments that befell the more unfortunate.

DUCKING

This is nothing to do with those sweet little quacking creatures...well, not directly anyway. Ducking was a punishment in which the offender was tied into a ducking stool and ducked (surprise, surprise!) in the moat or the village pond. VERY humiliating and VERY wet!

BRANDING

An immediate punishment for a wrongdoer was to have a burn mark branded on the body with a hot branding iron. The face was one of the worst places to be branded, because everyone could see that you had been up to trouble!

CHAINED UP

A prisoner could be chained to a wall with a manacle – a heavy metal chain with a locking iron ring. This was REALLY heavy and VERY uncomfortable.

Manacle

SMALL CELLS

Prisoners were often barred into small cells inside a castle. These had a stone bench seat, a small wooden door for passing food through, and not much else.

BURNING AT THE STAKE

This was a hideous yet popular method of execution during the 16th century. People who refused to follow the state religion sometimes met this fiery end.

A Frenchwoman called Joan of Arc was accused of witchcraft and burned at the stake in 1431.

HANGING, DRAWING, AND QUARTERING

This is really NOT one to dwell on.

The penalty for plotting against the king was to be hung, then have your innards removed, and finally...to be chopped up into four sections. Uuugh!

A PRESSING PROBLEM

Prisoners who refused to admit or deny their guilt were crushed to death... slowly! Each day, the torturer added more heavy weights to a board placed on top of the body. Squish!

PLAGUE

In the 14th century, a killer plague known as the Black Death spread worldwide and wiped out just about everyone who caught it. Here are some plague facts...for the more gruesome reader!

DEATH TOLL

It is thought that the Black Death killed a shocking 25 million people in Europe alone. Symptoms included skin turning black and a high fever.

THE GUILTY PARTY

The plague was spread by fleas, but they didn't do it on their own; they hitched a ride on rats. When the rats died, the fleas hopped onto humans. The humans caught the disease either from fleabites, or from other infected people.

A LACK OF PRIESTS

Around the time of the plague, people believed that it was important to make a final confession of their sins to a priest. However, so many priests died that most people had to be buried without prayers or a proper ceremony.

An Unlikely Cure

The gold and silver *pomander* below was filled with
sweet-smelling petals and herbs. The smell was supposed
to freshen the air and keep
the plague away.
Wishful thinking!

*Each section
had a different
herb in it.*

After the Plague

Life wasn't a lot of fun for the people who survived
the plague, although it was probably better than
being dead! So many people had been killed that the
survivors had to work much harder, and they didn't
get any extra money either!

HISTORICAL FOOD FACTS

Here are a few tantalizing historical food facts. Maybe you could memorize them and recall them next time you sit down to a family meal!

MIXED BLESSINGS

Festival time in the castle was a gastronomic delight, but the castle cooks did some weird things with the menu. Mixing sweet and savory things was common, so you could end up munching on roast heron, a sweet pie, fish, and dates – all in the same course. Mmm-mmmm!

OVERCOOKED

The remains of food were found at Pompeii in Italy, which was buried in ash after Mount Vesuvius erupted in AD 79. The not-so-tasty morsels included a loaf of bread, figs, and a bowl of preserved eggs.

LEATHER LUNCH

A band of 17th-century pirates became so hungry that they had to eat their leather satchels. A recipe left by one of them told of slicing the leather up, tenderizing it with stones, removing the hair, and then roasting or grilling it. An extra tip recommended serving with plenty of water!

Sailors called eggs cackle-fruit because of the noise the chickens made when laying. "Bacon, toast, and cackle-fruit" doesn't sound quite right, does it?

ROMAN DELICACIES

Want to try a change from your usual snack? Why not try out a dish described by one ancient writer – dormice cooked in honey and poppy seeds.

DEAD TASTY

Egyptian mummies had food buried with them (among other things) for the afterlife. Let's hope that they didn't have to eat too much of the tough bread that they ate in real life. It was so hard that their teeth got badly worn.

WHO ATE WHAT?

One of the ways archaeologists find out what people (and animals) ate long ago is by studying *coprolites* (preserved excrement). When cut up, they reveal fragments of plant and bone, and also eggs of infesting parasites. Oh, sorry...were you eating?

FASHION VICTIMS

Clothes have been worn for many thousands of years. There have been many weird and wonderful fashion items, but many of the makers and wearers became victims of their finery.

BELIEVE IT OR NOT...

Some of the earliest cloth was made from tree bark. It was soaked in water and pounded to soften it. Then it was oiled and painted, ready to wear. Comfy...NOT!

TAILOR-MADE

In medieval times, wealthy people employed a tailor to make their clothes. The tailor spent so much time bent over sewing in the workshop that a bad stomach and a curved spine were hard to avoid.

ARCTIC ATTIRE

Surviving in the freezing Arctic is a chilly business. It's probably just as well that it's cold when you consider what some of the traditional clothes were made of.

Jackets made from strips of seal or walrus intestine were popular!

BIG BELLIES

A peculiar fashion started in 16th-century Spain. Men had the fronts of their jackets padded with an artificial belly made from horsehair, rags, or wool. Very attractive!

PLENTIFUL PETTICOATS

Talk about fashion victims! In the early 1800s, a lady had to wear up to six petticoats under her skirt to achieve the right fullness and look. One of these was stiffened with horsehair.

WALKING TALL

So you thought that platform shoes were a fairly recent invention, did you? Around the 15th century, Italian footwear included chunky *chopines*, which were worn over shoes in wet weather. Things got ridiculous when some reached a height of 30 in (76 cm). Imagine tottering around in those!

SQUASHED FEET

Around 1,000 years ago, it became fashionable for young Chinese girls to have their feet bound up tightly. This made their feet painfully deformed, but small feet were considered beautiful.

SICKENING SNIPPETS

If you've managed to get through all the fascinating facts in this book and still have space left for more, here are some final snippets to complete the gruesome experience.

UNFORTUNATE INSIGHT

Giordano Bruno was burned at the stake at the end of the 16th century for saying that the universe was made up of millions of planets and Earth was one of them. Not far from the truth there Giordano! Bad luck!

A BAD MOVE

Colonel Pierrepont designed the first traffic island in Piccadilly, London. When it was installed, he stepped back to admire it and was killed by a passing hansom cab.

DEADLY TREASURE

Countess Arco of Austria found a chest full of gold coins in her garden and took it everywhere with her, strapped to the luggage rack of her coach. One day, on a particularly bumpy journey, the chest was jolted off the rack and fell on the countess's head, killing her outright.

DEAD PROFESSIONAL

Anne Boleyn, the second wife of Henry VIII, rehearsed her execution the night before. There's nothing like being prepared for the big event, is there?

KILLER BATHS

In 1903, two tramps were arrested in St Louis, Missouri, and were given their first baths. A nice experience you might think. Not really...both tramps died soon after this cleansing experience!

SPOOKY PREDICTION

In 1869, a lady in the court of the French emperor, Napoleon III, told him that she dreamed she had seen his state coach being blown up by a bomb...so the emperor never rode in his coach. It was probably just as well, since it was sold to Tsar Alexander II of Russia who was assassinated while driving in it in 1881.

INDEX

Acknowledgments: 95th Rifles and Re-enactment Living History Unit; British Museum; Chateau de Loches; Museo Archeologico di Napoli; Museum of London; National Maritime Museum, Greenwich, London; Natural History Museum; Pitt Rivers Museum; Science Museum, London; Viking Ship Museum, Oslo, Norway; Warwick Castle.

Picture Credits: (KEY: b=bottom, c=center, l=left, r=right, t=top) The Greenland Museum: 12; Scarab Pectoral, from the tomb of Tutankhamun, c. 1361-52 BC, Egyptian National Museum, Cairo/Giraudon/Bridgeman Art Library, London: 17t; Whydah International: 42b; Trustees of the British Museum:19bl.

Additional Photography: Geoff Brightling, Jane Burton, Tina Chambers, Geoff Dann, David Exton, Christi Graham and Nick Nichols of the British Museum, Peter Hayman, Dave King, John Lepine, Liz McAulay, James Stevenson, Jane Stockman, J. Tubb, Adrian Whicher.

Every effort has been made to trace the copyright holders. Henderson Publishing Ltd. apologizes for any unintentional omissions and would be pleased, in such cases, to add an acknowledgment in future editions.